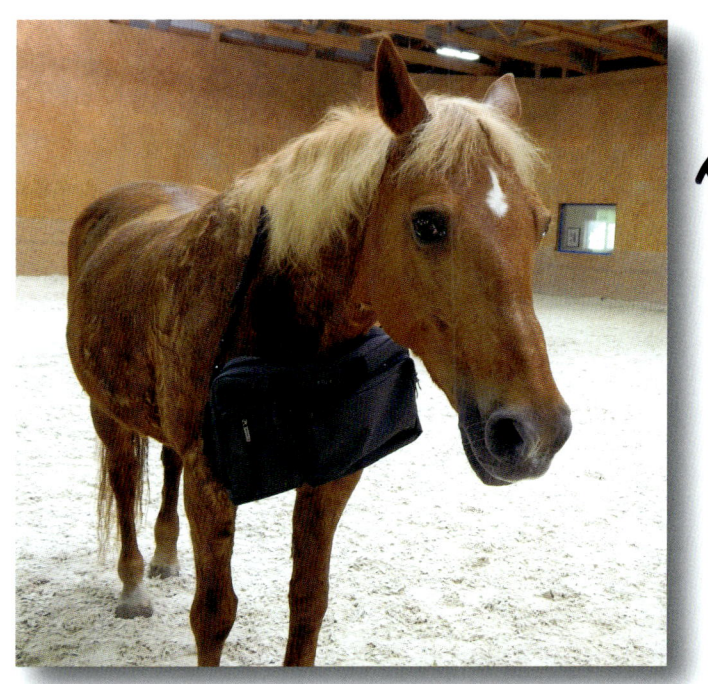

Bailey you are a [...] creation!
Casey Jo Conaway

Dedicated to those of you who helped me find my way home.

Once upon a time on a farm in West Virginia,
there was a horse named Choco. Choco was a very good horse.
Her friends liked her and thought she was smart
and pretty. One day, everyone began telling
Choco that she should go to college.

Choco wasn't very interested in going to college. But everyone kept telling Choco that college was a very good idea for her.

Choco liked living with her friends at the farm.
She didn't want to go away to college.

Everyone around Choco kept saying things like, *"You need to see the world"*. Choco didn't understand. She only wanted a little bit of the grass on the other side of the fence.

To please her friends, Choco applied to college and was accepted.
Everyone was so happy for Choco.

Everyone was smiling about the college acceptance letter. Everyone except for Choco. Getting the letter meant making even more decisions. What would Choco study?

People began to tell Choco that she should become a nurse.

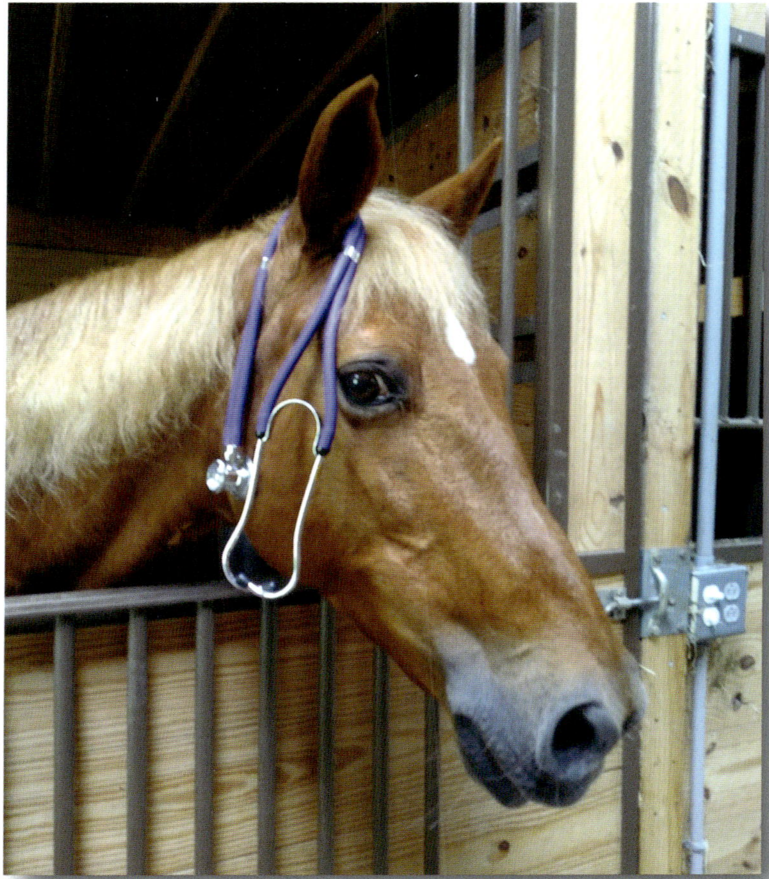

Some people knew that Choco was very good with food and thought she should become a culinary artist.

Other people told Choco that she was excellent with children, so she should become an elementary school teacher.

Choco was really good at comforting people and listening to them talk. Many people told her she should become a counselor.

When the day came for Choco to leave for college, she hugged and kissed the necks of all her friends. Choco was very sad, but everyone else seemed so happy. Choco kept her sadness a secret.

Choco went away to college and tried to become a nurse, but nursing wasn't for her. So she tried to become a culinary artist, but she liked eating more than cooking. After that she tried to become a school teacher, but she couldn't seem to get on the same level as the children. Finally, she tried counseling, but she did not want to talk with anyone so that didn't work. All of the trying made Choco's head hurt.

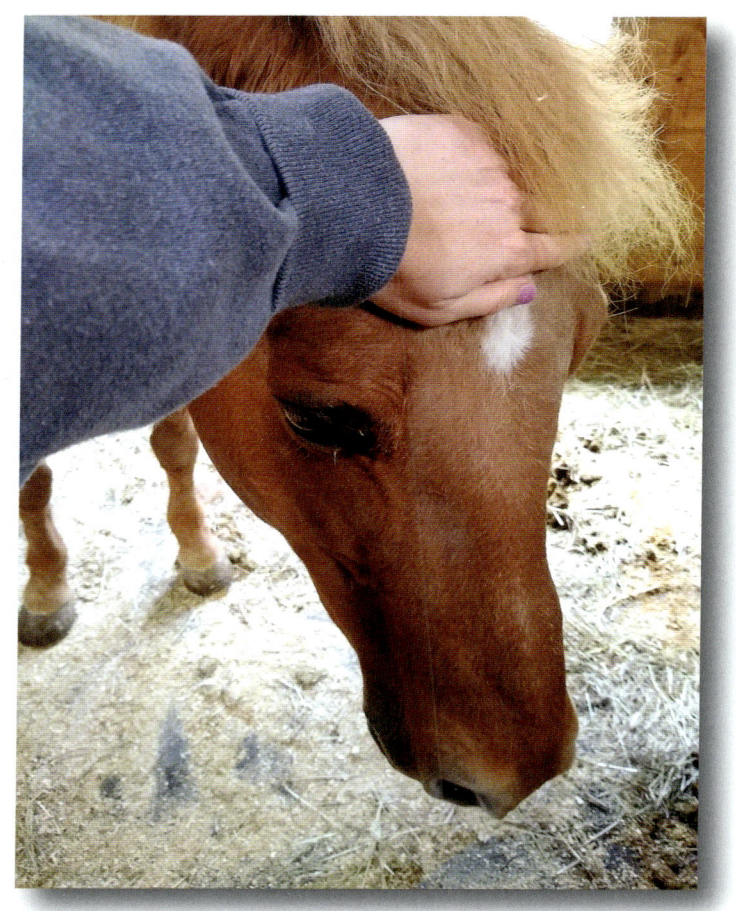

Choco performed very well in all of her classes. She made very good grades, but Choco was never as excited as everyone else was about her grades.

While everyone else celebrated her good grades, Choco was just happy to be home on semester break and away from school.

Choco tried her very best to fit in at college. She even changed her hairstyle to be more like the other mares.

One day Choco had to look herself in the eye and admit that college was not a good thing for her. Choco had to be very brave. Choco knew it was time to go home.

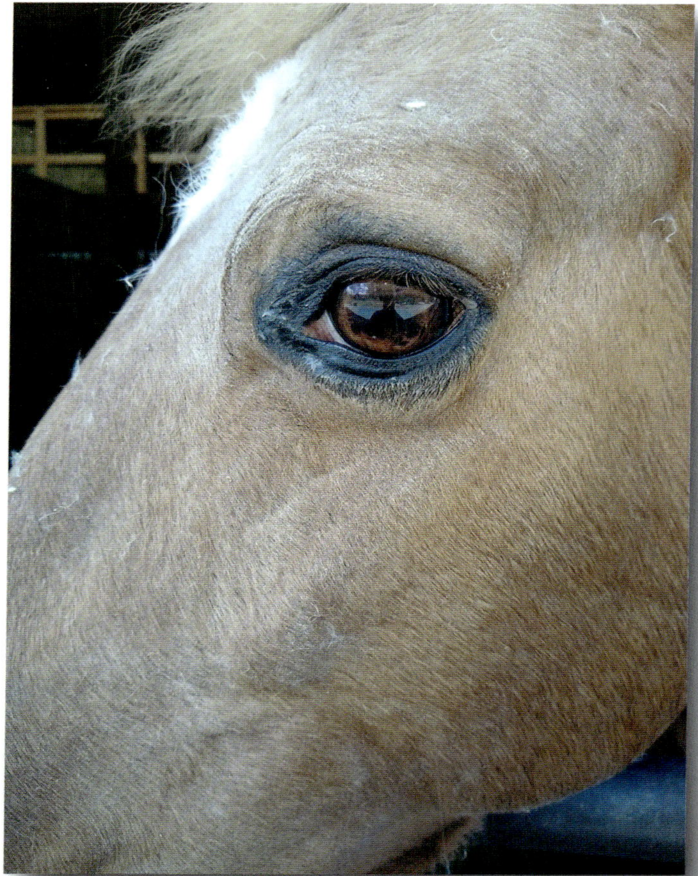

It was a long road home. Choco would take breaks along the way, but her feet felt like they were always stuck in mud.

When Choco arrived back home, she didn't feel well. She needed some help. It seems that trying to please other people made Choco a little sick. Choco's friends were worried about her, and they never mentioned college again.

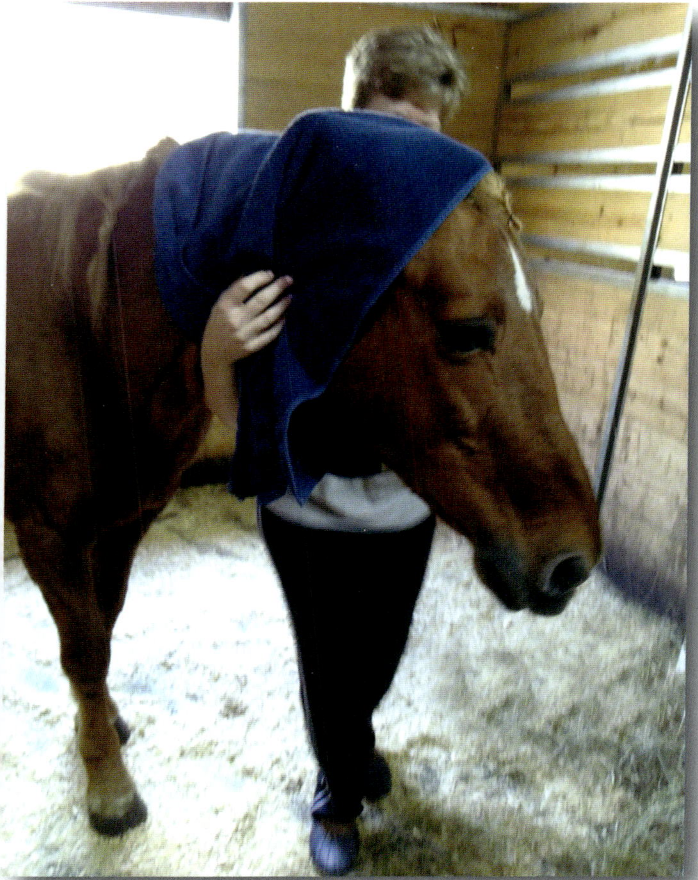

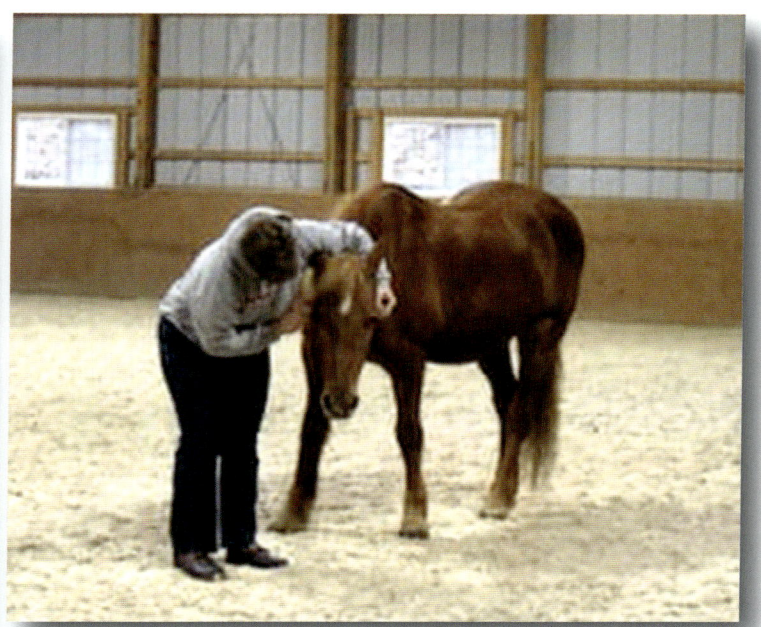

Choco saw a doctor, drank her water, ate her food, and over time she began to remember the way she was before she went away to college. Slowly, slowly, Choco reconnected with herself.

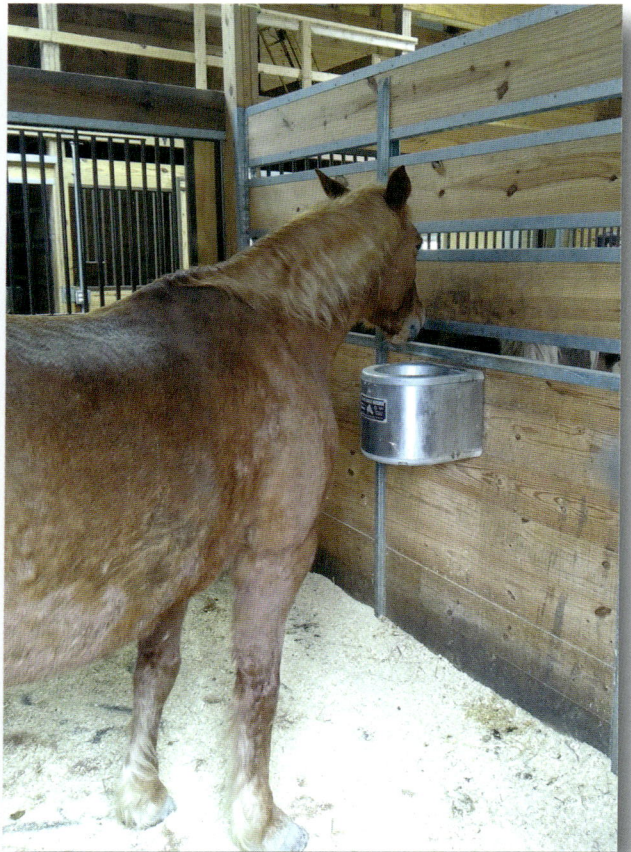

As Choco began to heal, she began to share herself again. Choco was always soft and liked it when other people were soothed by her beauty.

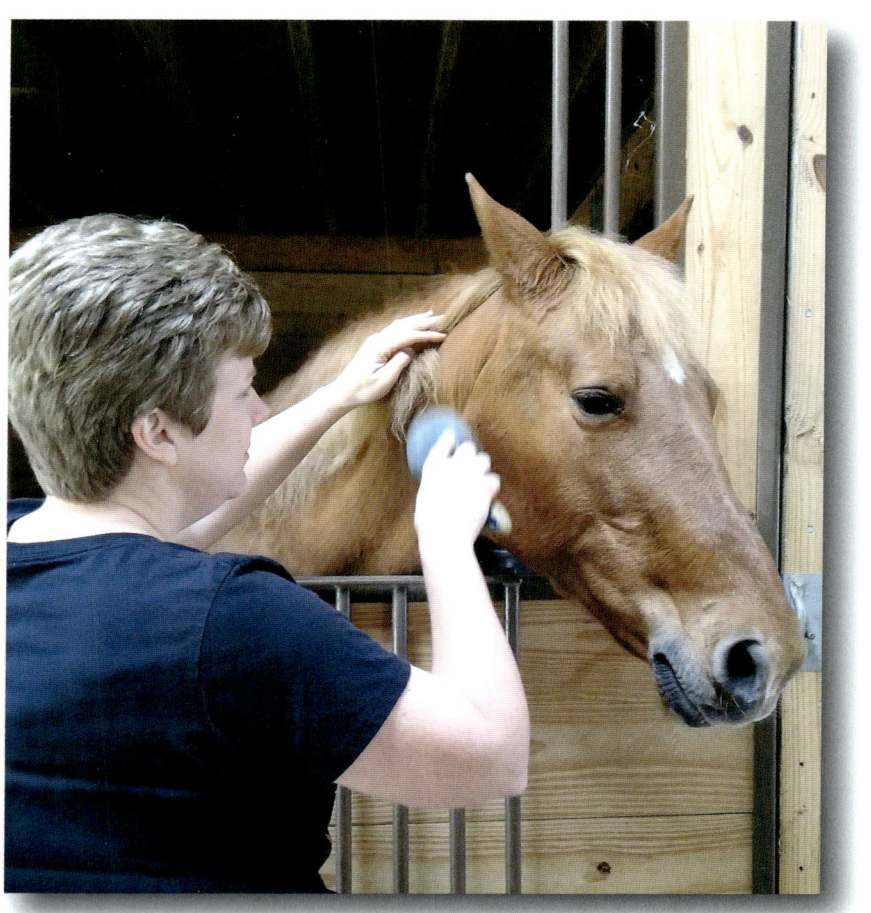

Choco was always known to be strong and peaceful. Slowly, she began to allow others to wrap their arms around her strength and peace again.

Because Choco had always been kind and patient, she would never leave anyone behind. Choco started walking with people again. Slowly, she started to understand that the Circle of Love had never stopped walking with her.

Choco wasn't any different from who she was before, but now she realized she had always been a good creation. Choco never left the farm again, and everyone around her was so happy that she was home.